S0-BFD-870

UNICORN RIDERS
We Ride As One

To my children and all those who believe in unicorns — AD
To my children, Clare and Max — JB

Picture Window Books are published by Capstone,
1710 Roe Crest Drive, North Mankato, Minnesota 56003
www.mycapstone.com

Library of Congress Cataloging-in-Publication Data
Cataloging-in-publication data is available on the Library of Congress website.
ISBN 978-1-4795-6548-1 (library binding)

When the Regal Conch is stolen, the Riders must find it before it's lost forever. Quinn soon discovers the thief is her evil twin sister Maram. Will the Riders be able to find Maram before she gives the conch to Lord Valerian?

Editor: Nikki Potts
Designer: Kayla Rossow
Art Director: Juliette Peters
Production Specialist: Kathy McColley
The illustrations in this book were created by Jill Brailsford.

Cover design by Walker Books Australia Pty Ltd
Cover images: Rider, symbol, and unicorns © Gillian Brailsford 2011; lined paper © iStockphoto.com/Imageegaml; parchment © iStockphoto.com/Peter Zelei

The illustrations for this book were created with black pen, pencil, and digital media.

Design Element: Shutterstock: Slanapotam

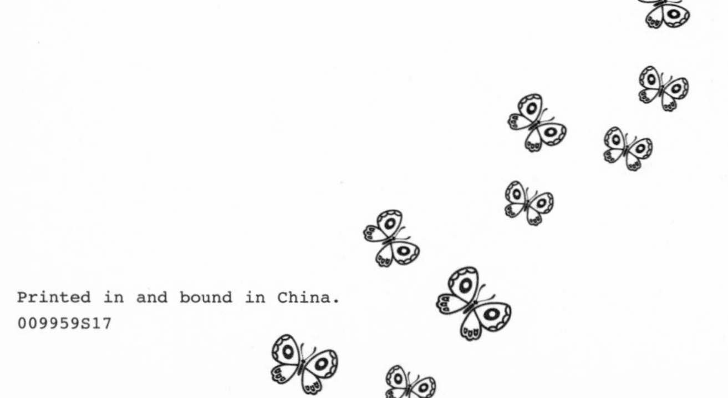

Printed in and bound in China.
009959S17

UNICORN RIDERS

Quinn's Truth

Aleesah Darlison

Illustrations by
Jill Brailsford

PICTURE WINDOW BOOKS
a capstone imprint

Willow & Obecky

Willow's symbol

- a violet—represents being watchful and faithful

Uniform color

- green

Unicorn

- Obecky has a black opal horn.
- She has the gifts of healing and strength.

Ellabeth & Fayza

Ellabeth's symbol

- a hummingbird—represents energy, persistence, and loyalty

Uniform color

- red

Unicorn

- Fayza has an orange topaz horn.
- She has the gift of speed and can also light the dark with her golden magic.

Quinn & Ula

Quinn's symbol
- a butterfly—represents change and lightness

Uniform color
- blue

Unicorn
- Ula has a ruby horn.
- She has the gift of speaking with Quinn using mind-messages.
- She can also sense danger.

Krystal & Estrella

Krystal's symbol
- a diamond—represents perfection, wisdom, and beauty

Uniform color
- purple

Unicorn
- Estrella has a pearl horn.
- She has the gift of enchantment.

The
Unicorn Riders' World

Kingdom of Obeera
Kingdom of Lillius
Kingdom of Korsitaan
Maylee
Trope
Mountains of Trope
Sea of
Desperation
Trilby
Kingdom
of Avamay
Palace
UR
Compound
Effervescent Falls
Desperation
Point
City of
Keydell
Stillmet
Tivia Wood
Miramar
Arlen
Cardamon
Hot
Springs
Islands
of Ipsus
Gringot
Merroweed
Woods of
Shanahan
Lake Feather-Lay
Dove Mountain
Dagger Mountains
Kingdom of
Haartsfeld
Gulf of
Curzon
Idle Bay
Sea of Angels

The Unicorn Riders of Avamay

Under the guidance of their leader, Jala, the Unicorn Riders and their magical unicorns protect the Kingdom of Avamay from the threats of evil Lord Valerian.

Decades ago, Lord Valerian forcefully took over the neighboring kingdom of Obeera. He began capturing every magical creature across the eight kingdoms. Luckily, King Perry saved four of Avamay's unicorns. He asked the unicorns to help protect Avamay. And that's when ordinary girls were chosen to be the first Unicorn Riders.

A Rider is chosen when her name and likeness appear in The Choosing Book, which is guarded by Jala. It holds the details of all the past, present, and future Riders. No one can see who the future Riders will be until it is time for a new Rider to be chosen. Only then will The Choosing Book display her details.

CHAPTER 1

QUINN CROUCHED BEHIND THE snow-covered pine tree, making herself as small and still as possible. One false move and she would give herself away. She glanced at Ula, her unicorn, and smiled.

That's it, girl. Stay quiet, Quinn sent Ula a mind-message. Like all unicorns, Ula had a special gift. Hers was the ability to communicate mind-to-mind with her Rider, Quinn.

You can count on me, Ula replied as magical sparks shimmered from her horn.

Quinn had spent the last hour searching for food in the forest. She hadn't gathered much, only a few small yams and a handful of winter greens, but at least she wasn't going home empty-handed. Alda, the cook, would be happy to have the extra flavors to add to her soups and gravies.

Quinn was still foraging when she detected a flash of caramel and white through the trees. Curious, she padded over the snow for a closer inspection.

Quinn watched as a spotted doe strutted past, unaware of her presence.

The doe paused to sniff at something below a thorn bush. There was a flicker of movement as a baby deer rose on wobbling legs.

Quinn gasped. It was still winter, and it was early for the doe to have a fawn. But there was no denying what she was seeing.

Isn't it beautiful? Quinn mind-messaged Ula. *So tiny!*

Ula nickered anxiously.

What is it, girl? Quinn asked.

Danger. Heading this way, Ula replied.

Quinn tensed. She spotted a gray wolf, nose down. It sniffed the doe's trail as it glided stealthily closer.

Quinn scanned the forest. She spied another wolf and another, creeping toward the doe from different directions. Their coats were shaggy and dirty. Their ribs were easy to see, as if they hadn't eaten for ages.

"We have to do something," Quinn whispered.

The thought of taking on three huge wolves was daunting. But Quinn couldn't leave the doe and her baby to their fate.

Before she even had time to stand, the wolves leaped into the clearing and surrounded the young mother and her baby. Their lips were curled, and their backs raised. They growled menacingly. The doe was too petrified to move.

Let's show them what we're made of, Quinn mind-messaged Ula.

You've got it, Ula replied as her magic whirled out from her ruby horn.

Quinn fought every desire she had to turn and flee. She ran straight for the wolves, waving her arms and shouting. Ula was right beside her. Out of the corner of her eye, Quinn saw the doe nudge her baby. Then they were off.

"Go on, get!" Quinn yelled at the wolves. "Get out of here!"

Beside Quinn, Ula twisted this way and that, alternately aiming her hooves then her horn at the wolves. With frightened yelps, the wolves tucked their tails between their legs and bolted.

"And don't come back!" Quinn shouted after them, excited from her victory, though her hands trembled.

Ula snorted. Quinn rushed to comfort her.

That was scary, Ula mind-messaged Quinn.

It sure was, Quinn replied. *Come on, girl. Let's go.*

Suddenly, the hair on Quinn's neck pricked. She felt like she was being watched. Thinking it might be the wolves returning, she spun around, scanning the trees.

She couldn't see anything.

I must have imagined it, she thought.

Quinn mounted Ula as Ellabeth cantered up on Fayza. "Look what I caught," Ellabeth said, flashing a string of silver fish at Quinn. "Alda's going to be happy with me. How did you do?"

Quinn held up her meager collection of withered yams and greens. "Not much food, but I do have an exciting story to tell you," said Quinn.

Ellabeth's eyes lit up. "Well, what is it?" she asked.

"Ula and I rescued a doe and her fawn from wolves," Quinn said.

"Wolves? Near Keydell?" Ellabeth asked.

Quinn shivered, sending her red curls swinging. "They were big and vicious, too," she said.

"You do seem pale," Ellabeth said, studying Quinn closely. "Are you okay?"

"We're fine," Quinn said. "It was lucky I had Ula with me. We stood our ground, side by side. I yelled and waved my arms. Ula charged at them, and the wolves scattered."

"Sounds like you had a lucky escape," said Ellabeth. She squinted into the distance. "Is that Belmont?"

Quinn's eyes followed where Ellabeth was pointing. A familiar gray and white falcon circled overhead. "It sure is," said Quinn. "Shall we ride back to the estate to see if he has a message?"

"Sounds good," Ellabeth said. "How about a race? Might make you feel better after your run-in with the wolves." With a flashy grin, Ellabeth took off before Quinn could reply.

"Hey, not fair," Quinn called after her.

Fayza was the fastest unicorn in the stables. Quinn knew Ula wouldn't be able to catch her. "We can still have fun trying, can't we, girl?" Quinn asked.

Quinn spurred Ula forward with a touch of her knees. The unicorn whinnied, galloping after Fayza.

"Let's hope this is the start of a wonderful new adventure," Quinn said, glad to be leaving the forest and the wolves behind.

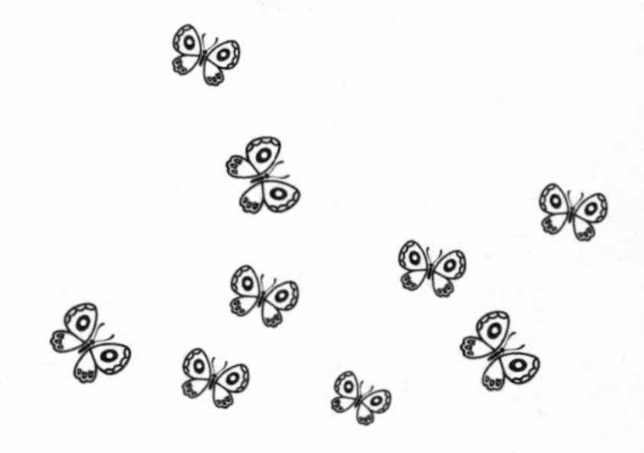

CHAPTER 2

BY THE TIME QUINN settled Ula into the stables, dropped the vegetables off at the kitchen, and ran up to the meeting room, the other Unicorn Riders were already waiting. Krystal was warming her hands by the fire, while Ellabeth flitted around the room, just like the hummingbird symbol on her uniform. Willow paced up and down, turning a tiny square of paper over in her hand.

"Is it a message? What does it say?" Ellabeth, impatient as ever, peppered Willow with questions.

"I haven't read it yet," Willow said, frowning at the door. "I'm waiting for Jala."

Quinn perched on the sofa's arm as they waited for Jala, the Unicorn Riders' leader. Krystal shot her a warm smile and hurried to sit beside her. "How are you feeling?" Krystal asked. "Ellabeth told us about your brush with the wolves."

Quinn waved her hand. "That was nothing. Ula and I are fine," she said.

"Thank goodness," Willow said.

The door opened. Jala strode in carrying four bundles wrapped in tissue paper. Each one was tied with a different colored silk ribbon: green, red, purple, and blue.

"Are they for us?" they asked excitedly.

"Hold your unicorns," Jala said, chuckling as she rested the packages on the table. "First things first. Willow, do you have something for me?"

Willow handed Jala the note. "Belmont delivered this," she said.

Jala scanned the letter before addressing the Riders. "Tomorrow morning, the Queen and her followers depart for the Council of Kingdoms," she said. "The Unicorn Riders have been entrusted with escorting the royal family: Queen Heart, Princess Serafina, and Prince Simon. The Queen wants us at the palace right away."

"Fantastic," said Quinn. She loved Prince Simon. Ever since their mission to rescue him from kidnappers, Quinn had developed a special bond with the prince. She liked the idea of spending more time with him.

Ellabeth, however, wasn't impressed. "I was hoping for something a little more adventurous," she said.

"The protection of Queen Heart and her children should be your top concern," Jala said. "I'm relieved you have an easy mission for a change."

"But adventure is my middle name," Ellabeth said, giggling. "Maybe we'll have to make some fun ourselves."

Krystal nodded enthusiastically. "Count me in," she said.

"Me, too," Quinn added.

"I'm glad you're as eager as always, Riders," Jala said. "I suspected the Queen would be in touch. That's why I had something special made for you."

"A golden carriage?" Krystal joked.

"What, so it can match your perfectly brushed golden hair?" Ellabeth teased.

Krystal sniffed. "I can't help it if my hair shines and yours doesn't," she said.

"It's not a golden carriage," Jala said, shaking her head. "You have unicorns, and there's no finer transport imaginable. Any other guesses?"

"You've had new uniforms made for us?" Quinn said.

"How did you know?" Jala asked.

"When I saw you and Tarrin Meyer, the tailor, talking in your study last week, I suspected something was up," said Quinn. "Plus, the packages wrapped with ribbons the color of our uniforms also gave it away."

"Brilliant detective work," Jala said, patting Quinn's back. "Mystery solved."

"New uniforms!" Krystal gushed. "Can I see?"

Jala handed each girl her parcel. Krystal and Ellabeth tore theirs open, while Quinn and Willow carefully untied their ribbons before peeking inside.

"Isn't my symbol the best?" Krystal said as she traced her finger around the diamond embroidered on her uniform. Each Rider's symbol was unique and reflected her personality. Krystal's diamond stood for perfection, wisdom, and beauty.

"My butterfly is better," Quinn said.

"You can't beat my violet," Willow said.

"That's nonsense," Ellabeth quickly countered.

"My hummingbird beats them all. It's so pretty and full of energy. Like me."

Everyone, including Jala, laughed.

"Each of you has an excellent symbol," Jala said, "which is why I chose them. Now, the Queen is requesting our company. You girls should get changed, and we'll be on our way. We're dining at the palace tonight."

The girls chattered excitedly.

"Yay, a trip to the palace," Ellabeth cheered. "That sounds like fun."

This must be important, Quinn thought with a nervous shiver. *I wonder why Queen Heart wants to see us so urgently?*

CHAPTER 3

QUINN'S FRESHLY POLISHED BOOTS squeaked as she strode along the palace corridor beside Jala, Willow, Krystal, and Ellabeth. She stared at the lavish gold and timber furnishings. Detailed paintings and tapestries decorated the walls. The statues and vases were made of crystal, marble, and silver and encrusted with gems.

Quinn had grown up in an orphanage. She had never seen such luxury before.

Imagine owning these precious things, she marveled to herself. *A single ornament would pay the orphanage's food bill for a year.*

Ellabeth elbowed Quinn, her eyes wide. Clearly, she was impressed, too. The Riders often visited the palace, but they'd never been in the Queen's private quarters before. This was a special moment.

A butler escorted Jala and the Riders into the Queen's dressing room. Queen Heart was gazing into a large chest and had a puzzled frown on her face.

"Really, Simon," the Queen said. "Couldn't you leave *some* toys at home?"

"No, Mama," Prince Simon replied. "I need them all."

Queen Heart spotted Quinn and the others. "My dear Riders," she said. The Riders curtsied as the Queen strode over to offer each girl a warm handshake. "As you can see, Prince Simon and I are discussing important matters of state. I assume Belmont delivered my message. Your new uniforms are divine, by the way."

"Hey, Quinn! Think quick," Prince Simon said, hurling a ball at her.

Somehow, Quinn caught it. She grinned and tossed it back to the prince.

"*Simon*," Queen Heart said as she wagged her finger. "Where are your manners?"

Prince Simon hung his head and shuffled his feet. "I must have left them in the kitchen when I was there," he replied.

Quinn and the others couldn't help laughing.

"Your Majesty, it's fine," Quinn said. "Really."

"It's lucky you have quick reflexes," Queen Heart said. "Simon does adore you, Quinn."

"You're very good with him," Princess Serafina said, stepping forward. The Riders curtsied once more.

"It's good to see you again, Princess," Willow said.

"I have asked you here because we have important business to discuss," Queen Heart said.

"Here is the itinerary for the Council of Kingdoms." She handed each girl a sheet of paper covered in elegant handwriting.

"It will take four days to reach Aster Valley in Korsitaan where the council will be held," Queen Heart said. "We will be accompanied by my soldiers. However, it will be your special task to protect the prince and princess. We can't have another kidnapping incident." The Queen hugged Prince Simon, ignoring his protests as she did so.

"Yes, Your Majesty," everyone agreed.

"Excellent," Queen Heart continued. "Now, there is one other thing I wanted to inform you about in person, rather than in a message, which might be stopped by spies."

Quinn's ears pricked up.

"The Regal Conch is a symbol of unity among the kingdoms. It's a long-held tradition that every council meeting be called to order by blowing into the conch," Queen Heart explained. "It will be your job to guard this conch as well as the royal children. Besides your unicorns, the conch is one of the most magical things in Avamay. Perhaps in all the kingdoms."

"Sorry, have I missed another history lesson?" Ellabeth asked.

"You would do well to listen better in class," Jala said.

"I listen," Ellabeth said, her cheeks flushing crimson. "It's just sometimes I don't hear. What is a conch, anyway?"

"It's a giant sea snail shell," Princess Serafina said.

Krystal pulled a face. "Minus the snail, I hope," she said.

"As you will see, the conch is rather large. The snail that once inhabited it lived to a ripe old age before it died. That was over four centuries ago," Queen Heart said. "The Regal Conch is infused with magic. Only the women of one family can touch it with their bare hands. These women are the Keepers of the Conch."

"The conch calls the kingdoms to order," Serafina jumped in. "By blowing on it, you can also communicate with and control the magical creatures throughout the realms. In the wrong hands, the conch could be lethal. Two people remain in the entire world who can hold it. If anyone else touches the conch, it will burn their flesh. The conch will then shatter, and its power will be lost."

"And those people are?" Quinn asked.

Serafina glanced at the Queen before replying. "Mother and me," she said.

CHAPTER 4

THE ROOM ERUPTED IN a flurry of questions. Everyone began speaking at once.

Queen Heart held her hand up. "Perhaps it's best if we show you," she said.

She marched over to a cabinet and unlocked it with a silver key. She took out a wooden box and placed it on the table. The Riders gathered around. Inside the box was a pink and apricot colored conch with a golden mouthpiece on one end. The shell was carved with images of unicorns, dragons, griffins, and other magical creatures.

"When the conch is played, the magic is released," Queen Heart explained, lifting the conch from its resting place. "You blow into the mouthpiece like it's a trumpet."

"What are the carvings?" Willow asked.

"Each one represents a magical creature native to each kingdom," Queen Heart explained. "Here is a unicorn from Avamay, a griffin from Haartsfeld, and a dire wolf from Zelbania."

"Is that a dragon?" Ellabeth asked, pointing to a carving. "From Obeera?"

"It's an eelios," Quinn explained. "It's a flying monster that spits venom and has wings that cut like swords. An eelios is smaller than a dragon but more powerful and deadly."

"Great," Ellabeth said. "Can't wait to meet one."

Queen Heart returned the conch to its box. "I'm surprised you haven't already," she said.

"Why?" Krystal asked.

"We thought they were extinct," Queen Heart said. "Now we suspect Lord Valerian is creating an army of eelioses to fight for him. Reports from my cousin, King Rhett, indicate that eelioses have been spotted in the skies near Lillius."

Lord Valerian was the evil ruler of the neighboring kingdom of Obeera. He had tried to invade Avamay before. He often made life difficult for the Unicorn Riders by causing wars and unrest. It was well known that he wanted a unicorn for himself. He was a dangerous enemy, and the Unicorn Riders always wondered when he would strike next.

"I don't like the sound of that," Quinn said.

"The conch must be protected," Queen Heart said. "If it falls into Valerian's hands, he will be able to call the remaining magical creatures from across the kingdoms to him. Those he hasn't destroyed already."

"How?" Willow asked. "Only you and Serafina can touch the conch."

"If the conch is returned to its seat of power on Fairisle, where the first Keeper lived," Serafina explained, "its magic can be reset so someone else can harness it."

"We won't let that happen," Willow said. "We'll protect the conch with our lives."

The others agreed.

"I knew I could count on you," Queen Heart said, smiling. Her slender shoulders relaxed. "Let's have supper. We have a long journey ahead of us. Proper nourishment is crucial."

"I like the way she thinks," Ellabeth whispered jokingly to Quinn, making her laugh.

The next morning, the Unicorn Riders trotted into the palace grounds as the sun was rising. Jala was staying in Keydell, but Ellabeth had brought her porta-viewer in case they needed to contact her.

Shaped like a hairbrush and set with orange topazes, the porta-viewer allowed Ellabeth to communicate with someone far away using another porta-viewer.

The unicorns pranced around. Their breath made frost clouds in the cold air. They were excited and nervous about the mission, as were the soldiers' horses.

Wagons were piled high with supplies and materials. One carriage stood out from the others, the Queen's gold and mahogany coach. Prince Simon begged his mother to let him ride his pony, Wisp, but she refused. She claimed he was safer in her carriage. Princess Serafina, however, was allowed to ride her horse, Riven, a silver stallion almost as beautiful as a unicorn.

The procession filed out through the palace gates. People waved and tossed flowers as the Queen passed. The Unicorn Riders received cheers. Their hair was soon littered with petals as the air filled with the scent of orange blossoms, winter roses, and lavender.

Quinn urged Ula beside the Queen's carriage and peeked inside. Prince Simon sat beside his mother, peering out at the sea of faces lining the streets.

"How are things?" Quinn asked.

Prince Simon's face broke into a smile. "Good, now that you're here," he said.

"You're safe with the Unicorn Riders, remember?" said Quinn.

Prince Simon nodded.

The Queen gave him a comforting hug. "Thank you, Quinn," she said.

They left the city, and Quinn fell back behind the carriage to ride with the others.

It's so wonderful being a Unicorn Rider, she thought. She studied the others for a moment. They seemed happy and relaxed. She knew they felt the same way she did.

"Do you really think this mission is going to be easy?" she asked Ellabeth.

Ellabeth grinned as she tucked a bouquet of lavender into her hair. "Easiest mission yet. Mark my words," said Ellabeth.

"More like, famous *last* words," Krystal joked.

"We'll see," said Ellabeth. As she spoke, the sky darkened. Snow began falling.

Willow shivered. "I'll be glad when spring arrives," she said.

"Me, too," Quinn replied. "I miss color."

Late that afternoon, the travelers stopped in a field outside the village of Trayneff. The girls sat around the fire chatting until bedtime.

“I’ll take first watch,” Quinn volunteered.

“Are you sure?” Willow asked. “You look tired.”

“I’m fine,” Quinn insisted.

Everyone went to bed while Quinn stayed beside the fire. Mesmerized by its warm glow, she stared into the shiny red embers. The color reminded her of her hair and that of her sister’s.

I wonder what Maram’s doing now? Quinn thought. *Is she safe and happy? Is she hungry or in trouble?*

Maram was Quinn’s identical twin sister. She led a dangerous gang. Quinn often worried about her rebellious sibling.

Before she realized it, Quinn had drifted off to sleep.

Some time later, she woke with a start. She shivered and glanced at the fire. It was almost out.

How could I have fallen asleep? she scolded herself. *I’ll be in terrible trouble if anyone finds out.*

Quinn studied the camp site. Everything seemed in order. All was quiet. She could even detect snoring coming from a nearby tent. She guessed it might be Ellabeth.

She trudged through the snow and woke Willow for her shift. Crawling into bed beside Ellabeth and Krystal, she fell back to sleep.

While she slept, Quinn dreamed she was riding through the snow on Ula. She heard wolves baying, as if they were hunting something. A deer and her fawn jumped out in front of her. The wolves were close on their heels. She couldn't stop in time. Ula neighed and reared, throwing Quinn to the ground. Throughout her dream, Quinn felt rather than heard Ula communicate with her.

Quinn, wake up. Something's wrong, said Ula.

Quinn sat up, her heart thudding. "Ula?" she gasped.

A scream cut through the night.

CHAPTER 5

"WHAT'S WRONG?" KRYSTAL SEARCHED for a candle beside Quinn.

Ellabeth, who was a heavy sleeper, grunted and rolled over. Krystal prodded her until she sat up, her dark hair ruffled. Ellabeth shoved it out of her eyes.

Willow poked her head inside the tent. "Riders, come quickly," she said.

"What is it?" Quinn asked, tugging her boots on.

"The Regal Conch is missing," Willow said, before running off.

The Riders made their way to Queen Heart's tent.

"I was attending to Prince Simon who had woken, asking for a glass of water," Queen Heart said. "That's when I found the conch box missing. It must have been stolen after I went to bed almost four hours ago."

"I've kept a close watch since taking my shift, Your Majesty," Willow said. "I didn't hear or see anything." She turned to Quinn. "What about you?"

"Er, no, nothing," said Quinn, shaking her head.

Quinn was glad the light was so dim. Otherwise, Willow would have seen her blush. She wanted to tell the truth. She knew she should. It felt wrong lying to Queen Heart and her friends. Worse was the thought of getting into trouble for sleeping on duty.

Quinn was overwhelmed with guilt. The Regal Conch was missing, and it was her fault.

"Without the conch we're lost," Queen Heart said as she cradled her head in her hands. "Fractures will erupt throughout the seven peaceful kingdoms. There will be fear and suspicion. Now, more than ever, we need the conch. Not to mention the magical powers it possesses."

"What I'd like to know is how does someone sneak in here and steal it from under our noses?" Willow asked.

"Must be experienced," Quinn said.

"Maybe it was someone inside the camp," Krystal suggested.

Ellabeth growled. "It could be more than one person," she said. "Either way, if I catch those rotten thieves, they'll be sorry."

"I thought no one could touch the conch," Willow said.

"You can if it's kept in its box," Queen Heart said. "You can't just touch it with your bare hands."

Quinn took a deep breath. *I have to say something. I have to confess,* she thought. *No matter what the consequences.* She stepped forward, about to speak, when General Barrella burst in.

"Your Majesty," he panted. "We found something."

The general led them outside. He pointed to a single footprint in the snow. "We think it belongs to the thief," he said.

"How do we know it isn't from one of your soldiers?" Willow asked.

"It's too small," Quinn said as she placed her boot beside the impression. "It's closer to my size. If not exactly the same."

"So we're after someone short," Krystal said.

"Not necessarily short," Quinn replied. "It could be someone young. Like us."

"Why aren't there more footprints?" Ellabeth asked.

Quinn held up a broken pine tree branch she had found on the ground. “Perhaps the thieves used this to hide their tracks,” she said.

“And missed this one footprint,” Willow said. “They were working in the dark, remember.”

“Riders, it appears that you have a new mission,” Queen Heart said. “Our party will reach Aster Valley in three days. It’s crucial that you locate the conch and return it to me before I make the opening address. The other rulers must not discover the conch is missing.”

“We’ll find it, don’t worry,” Willow said.

“How?” Krystal asked. “We don’t know what the thief or thieves look like or where they’re heading.”

“Perhaps Ula can see something,” Quinn said, closing her eyes to concentrate. The others waited while she communicated with her unicorn. “Ula says the conch is safe in its box,” said Quinn. “It’s definitely moving. She’s picking up one word.” Quinn opened her eyes. “The word is ‘wet’.”

"Wet?" Willow said. "Does that mean the thieves are heading for water? Or they're thirsty? Or it's raining or snowing?"

"Ula can't detect anything else. Just the word 'wet'," Quinn said, shrugging. "Maybe it means west."

"There's a distinct possibility that whoever has taken it will try to return the conch to Fairisle," Queen Heart said.

"Which is west from here," Ellabeth said.

"We must retrieve it before that happens," Willow said. "The thieves have a head start of several hours. We'll leave immediately."

"Wait," a voice said. "I'm coming, too."

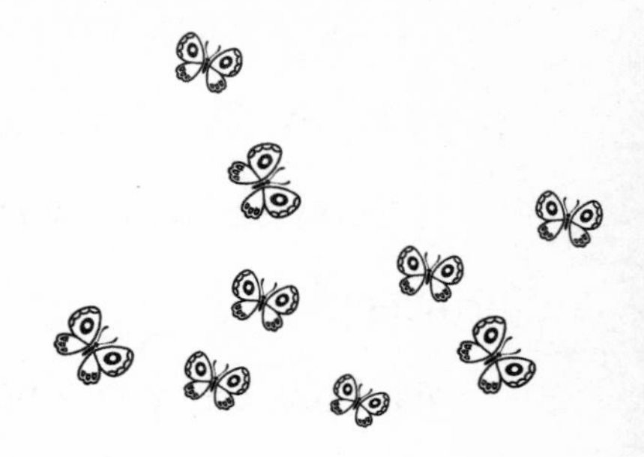

CHAPTER 6

PRINCESS SERAFINA STEPPED OUT from the shadows. "Please, take me with you," she said.

"We can't," Willow said. "You have to stay here where it's safe."

"I'll be safe with you," she replied.

"We don't know that," Ellabeth said. "You could be putting yourself and us into great danger."

"And the last thing we want is for you to get hurt, Princess," Willow added.

"I've been told that my whole life," Serafina said, eyeing her mother. "I can take care of myself. Really, I can. You risked your lives once before by getting the Dakkar scales for my armor. I want to prove to you I'm worthy. Please, let me come."

"Of course you're worthy," Quinn said. "You're a princess."

"And one day you'll be a queen," Krystal added.

"Being born into wealth and privilege doesn't make me worthy of anything," Serafina argued.

Quinn studied Queen Heart, wondering what she was thinking. "In our eyes it does," said Quinn.

Serafina crossed her arms. "Not in mine," she said.

"Even if you were allowed to come, your horse couldn't keep up with our unicorns," Krystal pointed out.

"Riven is strong and fast," Serafina said. "You won't find a better horse. Will she, Mama?"

The Queen nodded. "It's true," she said.

"Maybe," Serafina continued, "your unicorn magic could make Riven faster."

Ellabeth frowned. "Fayza's magic works only on unicorns," said Ellabeth.

"Have you tried it on horses?" Serafina asked.

"No," replied Ellabeth.

"Then how do you know?" said Serafina.

"I just do," said Ellabeth stubbornly.

"There will be no more talk of you accompanying the Riders, Serafina." Queen Heart was adamant. "Your place is here with me."

"But I'm one of the Keepers of the Conch," Serafina said.

"Under my guidance still," replied Queen Heart.

Princess Serafina opened her mouth to argue.

Queen Heart raised her hand. "Do not disobey me," she said.

Serafina's emerald eyes glinted with anger, but she didn't argue further.

"Take what supplies you need," Queen Heart addressed the Riders. "And be careful."

"Yes, Your Majesty," the Riders replied in unison. They raced back to their tent to pack their belongings before readying the unicorns.

"I think you've just got the adventure you were after," Krystal told Ellabeth.

"I sure did," Ellabeth said.

"Do we ride as one?" Willow asked.

"We ride as one!" the others replied.

Following the clue from Ula and clinging to the belief that whoever stole the conch might return it to Fairisle, the Riders took the main road west. Fayza used her magic to light the night and help the unicorns gallop faster. At each township they came to, they stopped to ask if anyone had seen anything suspicious or unusual. No one offered any clues.

"This is impossible," Krystal said, sighing.

"We're not giving up," Willow said. "We'll find them. We have to."

"Ula says the conch is still on the move," Quinn said. "It passed this way three hours ago."

At midday, they stopped at Bellnor to buy food and to rest and water the unicorns.

"Ah, you're back again?" the stallholder asked Quinn.

Quinn was confused. "Excuse me?" she said.

The stallholder pointed to the donuts Quinn was eating. It was her third one. "Like those, don't you?" the stallholder said.

"Ah, yes, I do," Quinn said. She didn't know why the man had singled her out.

Ellabeth nudged Quinn. "Never mind him," she said. "He has probably just been standing out in the cold too long. These donuts are good, though."

"You're probably right," Quinn agreed.

Still, she couldn't shake the feeling there was more to it. *Had the man mistaken her for someone else? Maram perhaps?*

No, it's not possible, Quinn thought. She and Maram in the same town? It was too much of a coincidence so she dismissed the idea.

The Riders finished eating and rode on. As they left Bellnor and continued west, a movement in the trees lining the roadway made Quinn turn. The hair on the back of her neck pricked. She scanned the forest.

Are we being followed? she wondered.

She didn't want to alarm the others, but something didn't feel right.

Ula, can you sense anything? Is there anyone in the forest? Quinn asked Ula through a mind-message.

It took a moment before Ula responded. *All clear*, she said.

Quinn sighed with relief. She must have been imagining it. Ever since she had lied to Queen Heart and the others about falling asleep, she'd felt miserable. She only hoped they would recover the Regal Conch before it was too late.

She urged Ula into a canter.

"What's wrong?" Willow asked, riding up alongside her.

"We need to get a move on," Quinn said. "I'm worried we're letting the thieves put too much distance between us."

"You're right," Willow replied. "Come on. Time to put some pace on."

The Riders continued until they reached a rocky gorge. A wooden footbridge, which would usually have been slung from one side of the gorge to the other, hung down the cliff face.

"This looks . . . ," Willow began.

"Suspicious," Ellabeth finished for her.

"Someone's cut the rope," Quinn said. Her stomach churned with fear. The conch was slipping further and further from their grasp.

"The thieves know we're after them," Ellabeth said. "They're running scared."

"Are they scared, or just running?" Krystal asked.

Ellabeth rubbed her forehead. "Either way, we have to get across the gorge," said Ellabeth. "We're losing valuable time."

"We can't fail this mission," Willow said, nibbling on a thumbnail. "I won't let it happen."

The others appeared so upset and worried that Quinn couldn't bear it any more. "Oh, this is all my fault!" she wailed.

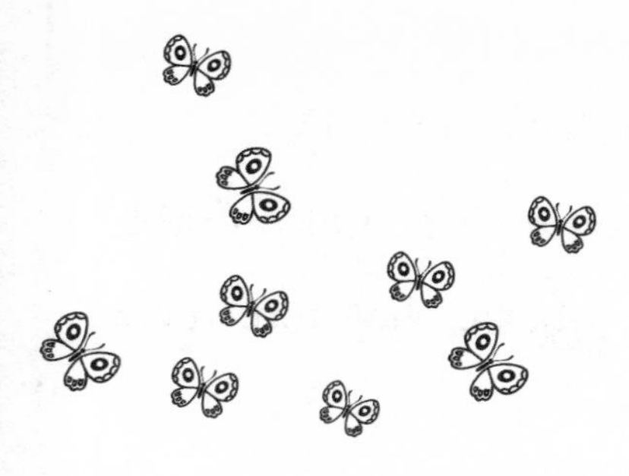

CHAPTER 7

THE WORDS HAD ESCAPED Quinn's lips before she could stop them. She had been feeling guilty for hours. It wasn't like her to lie or keep things from the others.

"Nonsense," Ellabeth said. "You've done some brilliant tracking, and Ula has been helping with her mind-messages."

"I don't mean that," Quinn mumbled.

Willow studied Quinn. "What *do* you mean?" she asked.

Quinn's cheeks burned. She turned away. That's when she noticed a scrap of cloth on the ground. "What's this?" Quinn said.

"A rag," Ellabeth said. "Probably nothing."

"The thieves could have left it here," Quinn said, turning the material over. "Maybe they tore their clothes when they crossed the bridge."

"It almost matches your uniform," Krystal observed.

"Hey, you're right," Quinn said. She wondered if it was important.

"What did you mean about this being your fault?" Willow pressed her.

Quinn gulped. Now that she was put on the spot, she wasn't sure she could confess. "Um, nothing," Quinn said. "I'm just worried. I really want to get the conch back."

"So do I," Willow said. "Well, we can't stay here forever. There's another footbridge a few hours ride south. We'll head there to see if we can cross the gorge. Surely every bridge can't have been destroyed."

It was a tedious and dangerous journey south along rocky mountain paths. They found the southern footbridge as snow began to fall. The wind picked up, howling between the cliffs as mournfully as a wolf baying at the moon.

Estrella pranced about nervously, unsettled by the wind. Krystal slid off Estrella and tried coaxing her across the bridge. The unicorn wouldn't budge.

"Use your calming magic, Obecky," Willow said.

Obecky sent gray-blue sparks of magic whirling from her black opal horn. Estrella settled enough to step onto the bridge. Her hooves clattered on the snow-slicked slats. The bridge rocked in the wind. Estrella lurched forward, skidding through the ropes and becoming tangled. She hung there, in danger of toppling into the gorge.

The frayed ropes creaked. "Help!" Krystal cried.

"Haul her up, Obecky!" Willow shouted.

Obecky's magic whirled. Slowly, she dragged Estrella upright.

The Riders hurried across the bridge, hugging with relief when they reached the other side. The unicorns nuzzled one another.

"That was close. How's Estrella?" Quinn asked.

"She's fine, but I have never been so scared in my life," Krystal said fighting back tears.

"We need to get warm and dry," Willow said.

"The conch is at stake. We need to keep going," Ellabeth insisted.

"I know what's at stake," Willow snapped. "But Obecky has depleted her magic, and Estrella is a wreck. The unicorns need to rest and eat. We do, too."

"Of course, you're right," said Ellabeth. Her cheeks flushed red. "Sorry."

Willow relaxed. "Right, well, I know a suitable place in the next town," she said.

It was dark by the time the weary group arrived at the Bloodhound Inn. They settled the unicorns in the stables, then fed and watered them. Obecky was so exhausted she barely ate.

As Quinn slipped Ula an apple, she noticed her backpack seemed lighter.

I'm sure I had more stuff in here, she thought. *Maybe something fell out.*

"Come on, Quinn," Willow called. "Let's go inside."

Quinn hurried after the others.

"Apologies, Honorable Riders," the innkeeper said. "We only have one room vacant. You'll have to share."

"That's fine," Willow said. "We're used to sharing."

Krystal groaned. "I need a break from Ellabeth's snoring," she said. "Are you sure you don't have a broom closet I can sleep in?"

The innkeeper laughed. "I'm afraid not," he replied.

Ellabeth plucked the key from the innkeeper's hand. "I see you're feeling better," she said to Krystal, as she playfully prodded her upstairs. "So, you'd rather sleep in a closet than with me, huh?"

Krystal shrugged. "You do snore," she said.

"How many times do I have to tell you? I don't snore," said Ellabeth.

"Go on, tell me again," said Krystal.

Shaking their heads, Quinn and Willow followed behind.

Everyone quickly washed up and then went downstairs for a meal. Willow, Krystal, and Ellabeth sent their new uniforms to be cleaned while they wore their old ones.

Quinn, last in line for the bath, told the others that she'd meet them downstairs.

She washed up then opened her backpack, rummaging around for her old uniform.

It wasn't there.

Quinn tipped the backpack upside down. Two green apples, some leggings, an undershirt, and a water flask tumbled onto the bed.

"Where is my uniform?" Quinn murmured.

She checked under the bed and in the other girls' bags, thinking they'd perhaps played a trick on her.

Nothing.

A nagging feeling tugged in her mind. *Did more than the conch go missing last night?*

She remembered the blue cloth she'd found at the broken bridge. *Was it from her old uniform?* The nagging feeling turned to dread. *Was someone else wearing it? Someone like Maram?* The donut seller thought Quinn had been to his stall before. Was it because Maram had been wearing her old uniform?

What is she up to? Quinn wondered. And *what will I tell the others? That I've lost my uniform? Or worse, that it's been stolen?*

Sick with worry, Quinn put her damp uniform back on. She made her way to the dining room where her friends were eating a meal of roast pork and vegetables.

"How come you're wearing your wet uniform?" Willow asked.

Quinn remained silent. She had to get to the bottom of the mystery first. She didn't want to blurt out her suspicions if she was way off. That would be foolish.

"Uh, my other one's too tight," Quinn said eventually. "I've grown out of it."

Willow piled a fork-load of carrots into her mouth. "Fair enough," she said.

Quinn couldn't believe Willow accepted her excuse.

She trusts you, Ula mind-messaged Quinn.

Quinn sighed. *Do you have to see everything?* she mind-messaged back.

Ula nickered gently, as if laughing. *Yes, I do. Now beware, someone you know is coming and needs your help.*

Quinn peered out the window. *Who's coming?* she worried. *And why do they need my help?*

There was no one there. All Quinn could see was snow.

My lies are like the snow, Quinn thought. *Piling higher and higher.*

CHAPTER 8

ELLABETH WAVED HER HANDS in front of Quinn's face. "Hell-o," she said.

Quinn blinked. "Sorry. I was thinking," she replied.

"Well, think about dessert," said Ellabeth. "Would you like a lemon tart or apple pie?"

Quinn smiled at the maid. "Apple pie, please," she said.

The woman disappeared and then returned with a slice of pie for everyone.

"That's what I call dessert," said Ellabeth, licking her lips.

Quinn peeked anxiously at the door as it burst open, sending a blast of frigid air through the room.

Snowflakes floated in and landed on the floorboards, making tiny puddles.

A traveler, wrapped in a heavy cloak stumbled in.

Is this who Ula meant? Quinn wondered.

Something about the traveler seemed familiar. Quinn realized the person wasn't very old or very tall.

The traveler plucked wet gloves off to reveal pale, delicate hands.

Quinn rose. "Princess Serafina!" she exclaimed.

The Riders rushed over and sat the princess in a chair. They unwrapped her soggy cloak and helped her to warm by the fire.

"Please, some hot food," Willow called.

"Certainly, Honorable Rider," said the maid as she hurried off.

Quinn kneeled before Serafina, holding her frozen hands between her own and blowing on her fingers to warm them. "Princess, what on earth are you doing here?" Quinn asked.

Serafina's teeth chattered. "I wanted t-to come on an adventure," she said. "I thought I could k-keep up, but we got caught in a storm."

"Where's Riven?" Krystal asked. "I'll get him nice and warm in the stables."

A tear trickled down Serafina's pale cheek. "I rode him too hard and tired him out," she said. "I had to leave him at a farmhouse. I've been walking for the last hour."

"Poor Riven," Quinn said, hugging the princess.

"I know I was stupid," Serafina sobbed. "I just wanted to help."

"You were very brave," Quinn said. "I can't believe you made it this far."

"Does the Queen know you've gone?" Ellabeth asked.

"I left a note saying I was following you," Serafina said.

"She'll be worried," Willow said. "Ellabeth, can you contact Jala on your porta-viewer to let Queen Heart know the princess is safe? Jala can send her a message via Belmont."

"Sure. I'll do it now," said Ellabeth.

"We don't have time to escort you home," Willow said. "You'll have to come with us. With enough rest, Obecky should be able to carry two riders."

"Won't I hold you back?" Serafina asked.

"A little, but it can't be helped," said Willow. "Part of our mission is to protect you. We're not leaving you behind."

The maid returned with some pumpkin soup as Ellabeth strode into the room. “All sorted,” Ellabeth said. “Jala’s sending a message to the Queen.”

“Thank you, Ellabeth,” said Serafina. She daintily sipped her soup, as a princess should. After she finished eating, the girls helped her upstairs.

“I know we’re all exhausted, so I think it would be best if we make it an early night,” Willow said. “I’ll sleep on the floor. Serafina can have my bed.”

“I don’t want to put you out,” Serafina said.

“We can’t have you sleeping on the floor,” Quinn chimed in. “Willow, I’m not tired. Why don’t you take the bed, and I’ll take the armchair?”

Willow raised an eyebrow. “Are you sure?” she asked.

Quinn nodded.

“Okay,” Willow said. “Thanks. Wake us in a few hours, and we’ll get going again.”

The others soon fell asleep. Quinn sat beside the window staring into the night.

I have to do something, she thought to herself. *I can't just sit here.*

A message from Ula popped into her mind. *Quinn, I need you.*

Quinn rose and crept down to the stables. "*What is it, girl?*" she asked Ula.

I sense someone important to you is nearby, came Ula's reply.

Is it Maram? asked Quinn.

I can't tell, but it is important you find her, Ula replied.

Quinn let Ula out of her stall. Together, they set off through the streets. They soon came to a night market crowded with people. Up ahead, Quinn saw a flash of red hair similar to her own. A strange sensation overcame her.

"I think that's Maram," Quinn said. "Quick, let's follow her."

Quinn pushed through the crowd, her eyes glued to the red curls bobbing up ahead. They inched closer until a wagon loaded with vegetables rumbled past. Quinn stopped short. The wagon splashed through icy puddles, spraying mud everywhere.

"Sorry, late for a delivery!" the driver said, tipping his hat as he sped by.

Quinn waited for the wagon to pass and then hurried on. She searched for the red head, with no luck. Her shoulders sagged with disappointment. "Let's turn back," she told Ula.

Rider and unicorn drifted away from the crowds. Footsteps thudded behind them.

Watch out! Ula sent a mind-message.

Before Quinn could react, rough hands pulled her into an alleyway. Behind her, Ula had a rope thrown around her neck, causing her to whinny in pain. Unicorns couldn't stand to be tied in any way.

"Let go of me!" Quinn cried.

"Not until you hand over the money," a male voice said. "We've got that boat waiting for you at Jesmora, and you owe us."

Remembering her martial arts training, Quinn stomped on her attacker's foot and elbowed him in the stomach. "Oof!" he cried as Quinn broke his hold.

She spun around. "Who are you?" Quinn asked.

"Nice try, Maram. Why are you dressed like a Unicorn Rider anyway?" the attacker asked.

"I'm not Maram," Quinn said. "I'm her sister, and I *am* a Unicorn Rider. That's why I'm with a unicorn."

The boy frowned uncertainly. "Is this a trick?" he asked.

"No, it's not. Release us or I'll have you arrested," said Quinn.

"Ah, no need for that," said the boy. His eyes darted left and right as he motioned to his companion. "Release the unicorn."

"What do you know about Maram?" Quinn asked.

"We're not saying anything," said the boy.

"Please, I think she's in trouble. I can help her," said Quinn.

"If she is in trouble, it's her own doing," said the boy. "We're out of here." Before Quinn could stop them, the boys sprinted away.

Quinn sighed. "I think Maram is the one who's stolen the conch," she said to Ula. "And she stole my uniform. I think she's pretending to be me."

She's betrayed her kingdom, Ula said.

"Don't say that," Quinn said, shuddering. "Perhaps I can find her on my own. Then I won't have to tell the others. I'm so ashamed of what she's done."

Isn't not telling as bad as lying? asked Ula.

Quinn searched inside herself and saw the truth.

"You're right. I must tell the others. Dishonesty hasn't got me anywhere," said Quinn. "Why does Maram have to be so bad? Why can't she try to be good for once?"

She's not like you, Quinn. And she never will be, Ula said.

Quinn knew Ula was right. The knowledge made her sick to the core.

CHAPTER 9

"I HAVEN'T BEEN HONEST with you," Quinn admitted.

She was back at the Bloodhound Inn and had woken the others.

"What do you mean?" Ellabeth asked, yawning.

"I've suspected for a while who the thief is," Quinn confessed.

"Who?" Krystal asked.

Quinn stared at her hands. "I didn't know at first, not back at the camp, but after a while I sensed something," she said. "And I started picking up clues. The first was the stallholder in Bellnor saying he'd seen me before. And then the piece of blue cloth I found. I think it's from my old uniform, which is missing. Lastly, when I went for a walk tonight, two boys claimed I owed them money for a boat at Jesmora."

Willow shook her head. "What are you getting at?" she asked.

Quinn took a deep breath. She hated what she was about to say. "The thief is my twin sister, Maram," she said.

Everyone was shocked.

"Why didn't you say something?" Krystal asked.

"Because I lied the night the conch was stolen. I did fall asleep," Quinn said. She watched the others for their reactions. "I understand if you're angry." Quinn hung her head.

"It wasn't your fault you fell asleep," Willow said. "Why didn't you just tell the truth?"

Quinn sighed. It felt good to finally get it off her chest. "At first, I lied so I wouldn't get into trouble," she said. "And then I kept my suspicions about Maram to myself to protect her. No matter what she is, she's still my sister. And now you probably think I'm as bad as she is."

Krystal hugged Quinn. "Don't be silly," she said. "You're such a worrier. Always trying to protect others."

"I thought I could stop her. I thought I could save her," said Quinn.

"This isn't about saving your sister," Serafina said. "This is about saving our world from destruction. Who do you think she's working for?"

"I'm guessing it's Valerian," said Quinn with disgust.

Serafina paced the room. "You said Jesmora, didn't you?" she asked.

"Yes," Quinn agreed.

"That's the closest port to Fairisle, which sits in the Sea of Desperation," Serafina said. "Where the first Keeper lived."

"And the seat of the conch's power," Krystal murmured.

"Right," said Willow. "We've got some riding to do. This is our last chance to cut her off before she reaches the coast."

It was midafternoon by the time the group reached Jesmora. Obecky was still weak from the day before. Carrying two passengers had slowed her down, despite Fayza's magic.

Up ahead, they spied a horse and rider.

"Is it her?" Ellabeth asked.

Quinn nodded, not taking her eyes off Maram.

She's nearing the boat, Ula told Quinn.

"Hurry!" Quinn cried.

The Riders galloped faster. Thunder rumbled as black clouds billowed across the sky. The gray ocean foamed. Waves churned and crashed along the sand.

Maram leaped off her horse. She dragged a small boat into the sea, threw something inside it, and started rowing.

"Is she crazy?" Ellabeth said. "She'll get killed going out in this weather."

Quinn sagged. "The conch is lost. We've chased her to the very edge of Avamay. We can't go any farther."

"We made a promise to the Queen," Willow said. "While there's breath in my body, we'll keep that promise. We must follow her."

Serafina chewed her lip. "Yes, but how?" she asked.

"We need a boat for us and the unicorns," Willow said, "and all the magic we can muster."

"And then some," Ellabeth replied, eyeing the storm.

They galloped into the town for help. No one would take them to Fairisle.

"That storm will rip a boat apart," one sailor mumbled. "The only water dog crazy enough to take you is Tarjack Salt."

"Where can we find him?" Quinn asked.

"On his boat, the *Ailish Dawn*. Down at the docks," said the sailor. "Never leaves the place."

The Riders found Tarjack Salt just as they'd been told.

"Honorable Riders," the sailor drawled when he saw them approach. "To what do I owe this pleasure?"

"We need to take a boat to Fairisle," Willow said.

"You girls know what a storm is, right?" he asked.

Willow nodded. "Of course," she said.

Serafina dumped a heavy bag into Tarjack's hand. "We have gold," she said.

The sailor shoved the bag back at Serafina. "What use is gold to me if I'm lying at the bottom of the ocean?" he said.

This is hopeless, Quinn thought. *He'll never agree to take us.*

"We'll take ourselves then," Willow said. "How much for your boat?"

"It's not for sale," he said. "Can't you wait till it's safe?"

"No, we can't," Ellabeth said. "The seven good kingdoms are relying on us."

Quinn stared at the old sailor. Her eyes pleaded with him to say yes. He was their only hope.

Tarjack growled. "Fine," he said. "I'll take you, though only Osara the Sea Goddess knows why. I suppose you want to bring those beasts, too?" He jabbed a finger at the unicorns.

"Yes," Willow said. "We need their magic."

"You're right about that, missy," he said.

As they pulled out of the harbor, the storm raged around them. Wave after wave crashed over the ship's bow. The unicorns stood on the deck beside their Riders, whinnying nervously.

Be brave, Quinn messaged while she stroked Ula's neck. *Everything will be fine.*

I'm not sure it will be, Ula replied. *I have a bad feeling.*

"I knew this was foolish," Tarjack shouted over the storm.

"Just keep going," Willow said. She turned to Krystal. "I'd ask Obecky to use her magic to calm the storm, but I know she's tired. Do you think Estrella can try her enchantment magic?"

"Sure," Krystal said. "We'll give it a go."

Pearly-white magic burst from Estrella's horn. It wove up and around and surged high into the sky. As her magic flowed, Estrella danced on her hind legs, trying to entice the wind and rain away from the boat and direct it to another part of the ocean.

But it was no use. The storm was too fierce.

Estrella dropped down onto all fours, her sides heaving from exertion.

"Never mind, girl," Krystal said, patting her. "You did your best."

The storm tossed the boat around as if it were only a tiny twig. The waves grew bigger and bigger until one crested above them like a monstrous blue claw.

“Surely someone will save us,” Serafina said. Her eyes were fixed on the ocean as if she were trying to find something.

“No one can help us,” Ellabeth wailed. “We’re going to die!”

“Hold hands,” Quinn said.

“For the last time, we ride as one,” Willow said.

The Riders, Princess Serafina, and the unicorns braced themselves. Holding hands, touching horns, they stood as the deadly wave crashed over them.

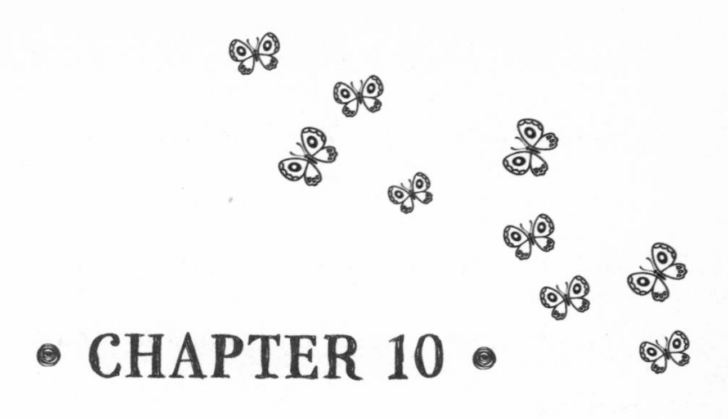

CHAPTER 10

THE BOAT PLUMMETED. THE RIDERS' hands were wrenched from one another's grip as they plunged into the dark, cold depths below.

Is this the end? Quinn wondered.

She fought against the sea's grasp as she tried to find the others. But she couldn't see, feel, or hear anything except the ocean's embrace. It twisted like a python around her, squeezing until the last of her breath fled her lungs.

Suddenly, Quinn felt herself being lifted. She shot up through the water. Gasping for air, she was thrust into the icy wind. Rain pounded her face and thrummed in her ears.

Quinn dangled high above the sea. Around her waist coiled something thick and wet. It squeezed tighter.

"What is that?" Quinn cried as she watched the limb coil around her. Terrified, she struggled to free herself of it.

She heard screams and saw the other Riders held above the ocean, too.

"Where are the unicorns?" Quinn shouted above the storm.

Ellabeth pointed. Quinn twisted around and spotted a rugged island coastline. The unicorns stood near a conch-shaped house on the nearby cliff tops. Serafina and Tarjack were with them.

They had made it to Fairisle. Almost.

Still struggling with the coiling mass that held her, Quinn looked down and saw an enormous purple head rising from the ocean. Her mouth dropped open in shock. Two huge eyes followed the purple head. Then came a vast black razor-sharp beak.

A giant octopus! That's what was wrapped around her waist. It was one of the octopus's giant tentacles. Realization hit her. The octopus wasn't hurting her. It had saved her from drowning.

Quinn was overjoyed. She was safe, as was Ula. And so were her friends.

Serafina waved her hands, seemingly directing the creature's movements. Huge tentacles set each Rider beside Serafina and then slithered away.

The rain eased, although the wind still howled.

"What's going on?" Krystal asked.

Serafina smiled. "That's Octello," she said. "He's an old friend of my ancestors. He rescued us from the storm and put us safely on land again."

"Were you controlling it?" Quinn asked.

"Not controlling. More like asking for help," Serafina said.

"Wow, I didn't know you could do that," Ellabeth exclaimed.

"There's much you don't know about me," Serafina said as she waved to the octopus. "Thank you, Octello."

The creature shrieked and sank beneath the waves.

Quinn was in shock. "What about the conch?" she asked.

"It's here," Serafina said. "I can feel it."

Then Maram has made it, Quinn thought.

"Is that the Keeper's house?" Willow asked, indicating to the conch-shaped building.

Serafina nodded.

Willow turned to Tarjack. "I'm sorry your boat sank," she said.

"It's okay," he said. "She was past her prime."

"What's that?" Quinn pointed to the sky.

Through the clouds, a dark shape emerged.

"Gredd's flying boat!" Krystal cried.

Terror gripped Quinn.

"There's Gredd," Willow said, pointing at the boat. "And Valerian is beside him."

"Come to do his own dirty work for a change," Ellabeth said.

Quinn couldn't believe it. She'd only seen Lord Valerian once before when she'd first joined the Unicorn Riders. He rarely ventured outside Obeera, preferring to direct his evil plans from the safety of his stronghold.

"It looks like we've got a fight on our hands," Quinn said. "Valerian wouldn't be here for nothing."

Beside her, Krystal shuddered. "Those soldiers are heavily armed," she said pointing to a group of soldiers standing on the flying boat.

"We can't let Valerian take the conch," Serafina said anxiously.

Willow's face set like a mask. "Don't worry," she said. "We won't." She pointed to some caves on the edge of the island. "Tarjack, wait over there until we return. We have some work to do."

Nodding and mumbling, Tarjack hurried away.

The girls and the unicorns stood resolutely, side by side, as the ship lowered toward the ground.

"Finally, you show your face," Willow addressed Valerian with her hands on her hips.

"What a shame it isn't under more pleasant circumstances, *Honorable Riders*," Valerian said as he dipped his head in mock salute.

"Why don't you come here, and I'll show you how 'pleasant' we can make things?" Ellabeth growled.

Valerian chuckled. "Brave words, fiery one," he said.

"Good to see you again, Krystal," said Gredd. A cruel smile twisted on his lips.

"Ignore him," Willow whispered. "Have Estrella use her enchantment magic."

On Krystal's signal, pearly-white magic flew from Estrella's horn, swirling over the ship. The soldiers' eyes glazed. Their weapons lowered.

"Fools," Valerian spat. "You waste your unicorn's precious magic. Cease instantly!" He flicked his hand. Red lightning zapped, dispersing Estrella's magic.

Valerian pierced Quinn with his gaze. "Tell me, child, where is your wayward sister?" he said.

Quinn tried not to flinch away from Valerian's scrutiny. "Gone," she declared, while her knees trembled. "And taken the conch with her. You know she cannot be trusted."

"Is that right?" Valerian murmured. "Then who's that?"

Maram appeared from behind the house dressed in Quinn's old uniform and carrying the conch box. "I'm here, my lord," said Maram, "like you asked."

"Excellent," Lord Valerian said as he smiled cruelly. "Return the conch to its rightful place inside the Keeper's house."

"Yes, master," Maram said.

"Stop!" Quinn shouted as she darted toward Maram. "I won't let you do this."

The twins faced each other. They had never looked so similar. And yet, they had never been so different.

"Do what?" Maram sneered.

"Betray our Queen and destroy Avamay," said Quinn. "Why are you doing this?"

Maram rolled her eyes. "Isn't it obvious?" she said. "I don't have the privileges you do. Instead, I do whatever I can to make my way in the world."

"Privileges?" Quinn asked. "I grew up in an orphanage."

"Huh!" Maram sneered. "What I'd have given for food and shelter. There were nights, days on end, when we didn't eat. Your precious Queen Heart never helped me. Why should I be loyal to her?"

"Ignore her, Maram," Valerian shouted. He threw lightning at Quinn. She dodged it just in time.

Valerian ordered his soldiers to attack. They began pouring down off the ship.

"Riders, get ready," Willow said. "It's time for some serious unicorn magic."

As Maram tried to push past her sister, Quinn caught her sleeve. "You're wrong about me," she said. "I've known hunger, too. And loneliness."

"Save it for someone who cares," Maram said as she wrenched her arm away.

Quinn's heart sank. "If you do this, I can't protect you," she said.

"You're the one who needs protecting," Maram said. Her grin was nasty. "Now, more than ever."

"Stop. I can fix this," said Quinn.

Open your eyes, Ula told Quinn. *You can't change her.*

The truth struck Quinn like a giant wave, drowning her with its cold reality. Determination coiled inside her. She grabbed the conch box, trying to wrestle it from Maram's grasp.

The first wave of soldiers rushed toward the Unicorn Riders.

"Use your magic to hold Valerian's ship," Willow told Obecky. "Krystal, Ellabeth, work with Fayza and Estrella to battle the soldiers while I figure out a way to defeat Valerian."

Over Maram's shoulder, Quinn could see the Riders and their unicorns working together. They combined their powers in an attempt to destroy the ship and overcome its occupants.

Estrella used her enchantment magic to daze the soldiers. Fayza used her light magic to blind them. Krystal and Ellabeth then moved in to disarm them.

All the while, Valerian hurled lightning bolts to break the unicorns' magic.

Quinn was worried for her friends, but she had her own hands full with Maram.

"Give me the box," said Quinn. "If you give it to Valerian, it could mean the end of our world."

"Would that be such a bad thing?" Maram asked between gritted teeth. "Maybe I don't like things the way they are."

Quinn was shocked. "How can you say that?" she asked.

"Because it's true," said Maram.

Quinn heard Valerian shout orders for the next wave of soldiers to attack. There were too many of them. The Riders were in danger of being overcome.

"It's not working!" Serafina shrieked. She ran toward the ship.

"Wait!" Willow yelled as she held her back.

"I can help end this," Serafina said. "Please, let me try." Serafina tore out of Willow's grasp, leaped onto the ship and threw herself at Valerian.

At the same time, Quinn jerked the box from Maram's hands. It broke open. The Regal Conch was thrown high, tumbling end over end into the air.

CHAPTER 11

"NO!" MARAM AND QUINN cried, staring at the spinning conch.

Quinn knew she wasn't meant to catch it. She knew if it touched her bare hands, it would sear through her flesh and then it would shatter. But she couldn't let it topple into the ocean and be lost. She had to try.

Quinn closed her eyes and held her hands out. A heavy weight landed in them. She braced herself for the burning sensation.

It didn't come.

Quinn opened her eyes. In her hands sat the unbroken conch.

Why aren't my hands burning? Quinn wondered.

An overpowering rush of magic flowered and then burst inside her. It flooded her heart, mind, and soul with awareness. All Quinn's senses turned inward as she absorbed the conch's immense power.

"How did you do that?" Maram asked. "Only women from the Avamayan royal family are permitted to touch the conch."

"I don't know," Quinn said, feeling different somehow.

With a blinding flash, she saw the truth.

I am of royal blood. The thought filled Quinn with pride, wonder, and confusion. *Where does my royal blood come from?*

"Blow it, Quinn!" Serafina shouted from the ship as Gredd dragged her off Valerian. "Blow the conch."

Quinn held the conch to her lips and blew. A deep, melancholy sound filled the air. She blew harder and thought about Octello. She hoped to gain his help just as Serafina had done.

From the depths, the huge octopus rose. He clambered up onto the cliffs, sending Maram and the soldiers scurrying back onto the ship. Octello turned his attention to the vessel, wrapping his long tentacles around it.

"Cowards!" Valerian shouted at his soldiers. "Attack that beast."

The soldiers ran forward to poke and prod Octello with their swords. The giant octopus squealed in pain, but he didn't let go. His tentacles lashed at the ship as the unicorns whirled their magic, still trying to control the soldiers and destroy the vessel.

Valerian shouted more orders. He flicked his hands. Red lightning flashed toward the Riders and the unicorns. The girls covered their ears against the noise and staggered backward from the blast. The unicorns whinnied in fright.

Screeches sounded overhead. An enormous, black shape swooped down at Octello. It spit venom and struck at the octopus with its sharp wings.

Quinn's mouth gaped.

"It's an eelios," Ellabeth cried. "Obeera's magical creature."

"Who's riding it?" Willow asked.

"Gelsen," Krystal said. She recognized him instantly. "Gredd's assistant."

"Eelioses are meant to be extinct," Quinn said.

"Remember what Queen Heart said?" Willow murmured. "Valerian must have been keeping one up his sleeve for this battle."

"Make that two," Quinn said as she pointed at another dark shape crawling across the sky.

This one flew down to Maram, who jumped from the ship's deck onto its back. Maram dug her heels into the creature's ribs and drove it toward the clouds. It hung there for a moment and then dropped toward the ground, firing venom as it went.

"Watch out!" Quinn yelled.

The Riders scattered. Quinn heard sizzling. Her sleeve had been sprayed with deadly venom.

Maram and the eelios dove again. While she attacked from the left, Gelsen attacked from the right. The Unicorn Riders were in serious danger. Red lightning and poisonous venom spurted and fizzed around them.

Once more, Quinn blew into the conch. She thought hard about the eelioses.

Stop. She tried communicating with them like she did with Ula. *We are your friends, not your enemy.*

The eelioses suddenly ceased screeching and spitting venom. A calm seemed to seep into them. They landed on the ground in front of Quinn, their giant black wings swishing to a halt. The ugly creatures tipped Gelsen and Maram off their backs and then bowed their heads to Quinn in surrender.

Without their eelios mounts, Maram and Gelsen were helpless. They ran to the ship and hid behind the mast.

Quinn kept blowing the conch. It seemed to give strength to the unicorns, making their magic intensify and grow. Gold, gray-blue, pearly-white, and pink magic surrounded the ship.

Valerian's magic was weakening. Octello, the unicorns, and the conch together were too strong. Valerian fell to his knees.

Gredd released Serafina and ran to assist his master. The princess climbed over the ship's stern.

"Hold the ship!" Willow cried. "Don't let them get away."

With the last of his strength, Valerian shouted an incantation. He flicked his hand at the unicorns, shooting blast after blast of lava-hot lightning a them. The unicorns stumbled and skittered backward.

It was all Valerian needed.

"You win this time," he panted as his ship lifted off. "But watch your backs. You never know when I'll return."

Valerian's ship quickly flew away. The wind eased almost instantly. A tiny slice of golden sunlight showed between the clouds and grew brighter. The battle was over.

The Riders embraced, and their tired unicorns gathered around them.

"Is anyone hurt?" Willow asked.

The girls shook their heads. Then they all spoke at once.

"Oh, thank goodness," Willow said, sighing with relief.

"I can't believe you caught the conch," Krystal told Quinn.

"Valerian has a lot to answer for," Ellabeth seethed.

"I'm glad you're all safe," Quinn said.

Over Krystal's shoulder, Quinn saw Serafina watching them. Once more, she was the shy princess she had been at her initiation ceremony.

• CHAPTER 12 •

QUINN TOOK SERAFINA'S TREMBLING hand. "What's wrong, Princess?" she asked.

Serafina shuddered. "That was . . . intense," she said.

The Riders pulled her into their group hug. "You did great. Just like a real Rider," Quinn said.

"Really?" asked Serafina.

"Really," they assured her.

"Why didn't Valerian just use the eelioses to invade Avamay?" Krystal asked.

"It seems his magic is strong," Serafina observed, "yet not strong enough. He needs the conch. That's why he sent Maram to steal it."

"Why is Quinn able to touch it?" Ellabeth asked.

"She must possess royal blood," Serafina said. "Somewhere in the past, her family line joins mine. We're related."

Quinn blushed with happiness. "Who would have thought? Me, a royal!" she said.

"Has the conch given you magic?" Quinn asked Serafina.

"Yes," Serafina said. "My magic is connected to the conch. I would lose it if the conch were destroyed."

"What about Queen Heart?" Quinn asked. "Has the conch given her magic?"

"A little, though not as much," Serafina said. "I can communicate with Octello and other creatures, while she can't. What about you?"

"I felt its magic flow through me. Somehow I feel . . . different," said Quinn.

"Over time your powers will grow," Serafina said with a smile.

"What type of powers?" Krystal asked.

"It's different for everyone," Serafina said. "My magic helped me travel faster when I was following you."

"I wondered how you caught up to us so quickly," Willow said.

"That's just great," Ellabeth snorted. "Not only does she have royalty in her veins, now she has magic, too. Some people get all the breaks."

Everyone laughed.

"What will Queen Heart think when she finds out?" Krystal asked.

"She'll be thrilled," Serafina replied.

Quinn blushed even harder until realization struck her. "This also means Maram can control the conch," she said.

"Which makes her more dangerous than ever," Ellabeth said.

Quinn shuddered. "I can't bear to think about it," she said.

"We don't have to worry about that right away," Willow said. "But we do need to return the conch to Queen Heart."

"Is this a private party or can anyone join in?" said a man's voice.

The group turned to see Tarjack.

"Tarjack, are you okay?" Krystal asked.

"Nope," Tarjack said. "I will never be the same again."

"What's wrong?" Ellabeth asked. Concerned, the girls gathered around him.

"Nothing like that," he said, sniffing and swiping at his eyes. "I mean, after what I saw, the way you and the unicorns worked to fight Valerian. I'm lost for words to describe it."

"Are you crying?" Ellabeth asked.

"Nah. I don't cry," he said.

"This is all in a day's work for us," Krystal assured him. "We're lucky we've got the unicorns."

"Don't forget Octello," Serafina said.

"We didn't thank him." Willow searched for the giant octopus, but he had disappeared.

"He knows we're grateful," Serafina said.

"How are we going to get the conch to Queen Heart?" Ellabeth asked. "We don't have much time before the Council of Kingdom starts."

Quinn's eyes lit up. "Perhaps we can harness the magic of the conch to help us. It energized the unicorns before," said Quinn.

"Great idea," Serafina said. "Let's give it a try."

"First, I have to take care of something," Quinn said. She blew into the conch. The eelioses lifted their heads. They weren't so terrifying any more. Now they seemed more like giant puppy dogs, not venom-spitting demons.

"This is your new home," Quinn said. "Stay here where you're safe from Valerian and away from his influence.

One day we might need you to help us. You can roost in those caves."

The eelioses screeched then took off toward the caves.

"How will we get back to Jesmora without a boat?" Krystal asked.

As if on cue, Octello rose from the ocean holding something in one of his tentacles.

"My *Ailish Dawn*!" Tarjack cried with joy.

Octello drained the water from the boat and then placed it on the ocean. One by one, he placed the Riders, Serafina, Tarjack, and the unicorns onto the deck.

The octopus gave the boat a push toward Avamay.

"Hooray for Octello!" Ellabeth cheered, and the others joined in.

At Jesmora, the Riders and Serafina said goodbye to Tarjack. Then, with the help of the conch, they set off at double speed.

"Do you think we'll make it?" Quinn asked Willow as they raced along.

"Seven kingdoms are depending on us," Willow replied. "We have to make it."

With the power of the conch, it took them only a day to reach Korsitaan. As they rode up and over the mountain range surrounding Aster Valley, the Riders halted the unicorns. Row after row of white tents were spread out below.

"Wow, our first Council of Kingdoms," Krystal breathed. "Isn't it exciting?"

"It sure is," Quinn said, staring down into the valley, knowing she'd changed. She felt magic budding inside her. But more than that, she felt peace and confidence. "I wish Jala could be here."

"I can fix that," Ellabeth said as she handed her the porta-viewer. "She'll want to know what's happening. Why don't you do the honors?"

"What, now?" asked Quinn.

"Yes, now. Go on," Ellabeth said.

Quinn opened the porta-viewer. Jala appeared immediately. "Quinn," she said. "It's so good to see you. How are things?"

"Everything's fine. We just wanted to let you know we recovered the conch," said Quinn. "We're about to return it to Queen Heart."

"Excellent," Jala said. "Is the princess safe?"

"Which one?" Ellabeth joked.

"Pardon?" Jala asked.

Quinn coughed. "It's a long story," she said. "I'll tell you when we get home. But what I can say is that I learned a few things about myself on this mission."

"Good for you," Jala said. "I can't wait to hear all about it. At the moment, I have a feeling you're needed elsewhere."

Jala signed off. Quinn closed the porta-viewer.

I'm proud of you, Ula's voice echoed in her mind.

Thanks, Ula, Quinn replied.

Without warning, a flash of light erupted before Quinn's eyes. A vision emerged, blurry at first and then growing clearer.

Two girls, so similar, yet so different, faced each other on a battlefield.

A chill swept along Quinn's arms, making the hairs stand on end.

So that is how it will be, she thought.

Quinn's vision evaporated. She shook her head to clear it.

In the valley below, a stage had been built. Every head of state from the peaceful kingdoms was gathered there. The kingdoms were Avamay, Lillius, Korsitaan, Haartsfeld, Calbeeda, Zelbania, and Purrillo.

Queen Heart rose to take the podium. Quinn saw her turn her worried face toward the mountains.

"She's looking for us," Quinn said.

Willow smiled. "Well, we'd better get down there. Do we ride as one?" Willow asked.

The Riders' reply was strong and clear. "We ride as one!"

Glossary

coincidence (koh-IN-si-duhns)—something that happens accidentally at the same time as something else

daunting (DAWNT-ing)—frightening or discouraging

extinct (ik-STINGKT)—when a species no longer exists on Earth

fate (FATE)—a force that some believe controls events and people's lives; destiny

forage (FOR-ij)—to go in search of food

immense (i-MENS)—extremely large

itinerary (eye-TIN-uh-rer-ee)—a plan for a trip

lethal (LEE-thuhl)—very harmful or deadly

meager (MEE-gur)—very small, or not enough

orphanage (OR-fuh-nij)—a place where orphans live and are cared for

petrified (PET-ruh-fide)—a material that has been changed into stone or a stony substance by water and minerals

privilege (PRIV-uh-lij)—a special right or advantage given to a person or a group of people

rebellious (ri-BEL-yuhss)—struggling against the people in charge

venom (VEN-uhm)—harmful liquid produced by some animals to kill or injure another animal

wayward (WAYWARD)—not following a rule or regular course of action

Discussion Questions

1. What are some examples of how Quinn showed courage throughout the story?
2. Do you think Princess Serafina will go on future missions with the Riders? Why or why not?
3. Why did Quinn put off telling the other Riders about her suspicions that Maram was the thief?

Writing Prompts

1. If you were a Unicorn Rider, what symbol do you think Jala would give you? Why?
2. Why do you think Quinn wanted to help her sister Maram so badly? Do you think she ever will be able to help her?
3. What do you think Quinn will do with the powers that she received from the conch?

UNICORN RIDERS

COLLECT THE SERIES!